How to Hide a Lion from Grandma

If yo

Helen Stephens

There was once a lion who lived with a little girl called Iris.
He was a brave, kind lion, who had saved the Mayor's
best candlesticks from some robbers.

He was the town hero,
and Iris loved him.

However, one weekend, Grandma was coming to stay while Iris's mum and dad went away. The lion would have to hide, as grandmas can get anxious if they find a lion in the house.

But where could he go?

Behind the curtains?

Under Grandma's bed?

It wasn't going to be easy.

Iris loved her grandma. She always brought interesting things with her. This time, she brought an absolutely

enormous box.

"It's just a few hats and bits and bobs!" said Grandma.

"They're very **heavy** hats and bits and bobs," grumbled Mum and Dad, as they heaved the box upstairs to Grandma's bedroom.

But Iris was excited.

"Can we play dressing up?" she said.

"We'll see," said Grandma. She never even spotted the lion. She just thought he was a coat stand.

In fact, it turned out to be quite easy hiding the lion from Grandma, because she was so short-sighted. First, she thought he was a lamp.

Then she thought he was a towel.

She even mistook
him for a sofa.

She never even noticed when the lion sneaked behind them all the way to the supermarket.

"Ah, tuna!" said Grandma, and she piled twenty-two tins into the trolley. Plus forty-three pints of milk, two dozen French sticks, fifteen bunches of bananas, fifty-seven jars of honey and forty pots of crunchy peanut butter.

"What a lot of food," said Iris.

Grandma explained that
she often got peckish in the night.

On the bus home, Iris asked if they could play with the great big dressing-up box when they got back, but Grandma just said, "We'll see."

And in the end there wasn't time, as Grandma spent so long making mountains and mountains of sandwiches.

"I do like a little snack at bedtime," she said, and she took the whole tray up to her bedroom.

Later, when Iris should have been asleep, she heard some strange sounds coming from Grandma's bedroom.

The lion tried to pull her away.

"It's only Grandma, having a snack," said Iris.

But did Grandma normally make those noises?

Iris peered through the keyhole. What **was** Grandma doing?

She wasn't eating the sandwiches at all – she was tipping them into the great big dressing-up box!

Iris and the lion didn't know what to make of it. There was definitely something funny about that box. Iris couldn't ask Grandma now, because she was supposed to be fast asleep.

"I'll ask her first thing in the morning," she said.

Very early next morning, Iris woke Grandma up. "I have to see inside your dressing-up box," she said.

But Grandma said it was too early, and she went back to sleep.

Iris couldn't wait, though. She tiptoed over and listened.
She heard snuffling. And snoring.

Whatever was inside that box,
it wasn't just hats and bits and bobs!

Iris climbed up to take a look. The lion was worried. He gave a little whimper.

"Shhh!" whispered Iris.
"You'll wake Grandma."

She heaved the huge lid open, and peeped in. There was something furry in there.

And it growled!

The lion pounced at the box.
ROAR!
It tipped right over,
and out tumbled . . .

a bear!

All that noise woke Grandma up.

"Good heavens!" she said. "You've found Bernard!

And, gracious!" said Grandma. "Is that a **lion**?

Where on earth has **he** been hiding?"

Bernard was a very friendly bear. He gave everyone bear hugs.

"I thought you'd be frightened of him," said Grandma.

"I thought you'd be frightened of my lion," said Iris.

Then they all played dressing up
with the hats and bits and bobs,
which had tumbled out of
the box as well.

"Bernard loves dressing
up," said Grandma.

All of a sudden, they heard a car pull up outside.
"Quick!" said Grandma. "Mum and Dad are back!
Let's surprise them!"

So they all hid behind the sofa, and Iris went, "Shhh!"

Then, when Mum and Dad came through the door, they all went . . .

And Mum and Dad were **very** surprised!

First published in the UK in 2014 by
Alison Green Books
An imprint of Scholastic Children's Books
Euston House, 24 Eversholt Street
London NW1 1DB, UK
A division of Scholastic Ltd
www.scholastic.co.uk
London – New York – Toronto – Sydney – Auckland
Mexico City – New Delhi – Hong Kong

HB ISBN: 978 1 407139 04 3
PB ISBN: 978 1 407139 05 0

Printed in Malaysia.

10 9 8 7 6 5 4 3 2

Papers used by Scholastic Children's Books are made
from wood grown in sustainable forests.

For Frieda, the real-life Iris